CHAPTER *one

I stood on stage, under the spotlight. Even though the rest of the concert hall was in darkness I knew that it was full of people, watching me. But I wasn't nervous at all. I'd practised this dance routine hundreds of times. I knew I wouldn't make a mistake.

The music started and I began dancing. My costume trailed behind me like mist as I moved. I had to be careful that I didn't step on it. It would be terrible to fall over in front of all these people. But I didn't fall, even when the music became really fast.

The hardest part was towards the end when I had to spin five times in a row, then jump into the air. I started spinning and the spotlight followed me across the stage. By the third twirl I knew everything was going to be OK.

I finished with the splits and the crowd went wild. They rose to their feet and cheered. My best friend, Dani, ran on to the stage and gave me a big hug.

'That was really cool, Chloe,' she said.

As she spoke, the concert hall and all the people disappeared.

We were in Dani's sitting room.

'I think our dance routine is looking great,' Dani added.

'Me, too,' I said.

Dani and I had been working on this routine all summer. Dani did dance lessons, so she worked out most of it. But I had made up a few steps, too, which Dani said were really good.

After our practice, we were both pooped. We flopped down on to the floor, still in our costumes. Dani's mum had given us a bag of old stuff to use. I was wearing a soft silky dress covered in tiny gold beads. It was excellent to dance in because it swirled out around me when

I spun. Dani's outfit was a satin skirt with a zebra pattern. It was too big so to keep it up she had on a wide stretchy belt.

'Can you believe it's the last day of the holidays?' said Dani.

I shook my head. 'This summer has gone so fast,' I said.

'I'm actually looking forward to going back,' Dani admitted. 'Is that weird?'

I knew what she meant. It had been a great holiday, but I was also excited about going back to school.

Everything was going to change this year. We were moving to a whole new area, where the older kids go. There would be different classrooms, different toilets.

I'm actually looking forward to going back to school!

There would even be a different playground. It was almost like starting at a new school.

'But I'm a bit nervous, too,' Dani said. 'Everyone says the work will be much harder now. Especially maths.'

I got butterflies in my stomach when she said that. Maths wasn't exactly my best subject. I had done OK in Mrs Khan's class last year, but the work was pretty easy.

'I think it depends on which teacher

you get,' I said. 'Mr Stavros is nice but Mrs Clarke is really strict.'

My big sister, Ashley, used to go to the same school as me. She'd told me all about the teachers.

'Mr Stavros gives out stickers if you do good work,' she said. 'But Mrs Clarke only ever gives ticks. And no one ever gets more than one tick.'

I wanted to be in Mr Stavros's class. He played the guitar and gave his pupils silly nicknames. There was a boy in his class last year called Alec Jamieson but Mr Stavros called him 'I-lick-jam-and-scones'. It was a bit silly, but it was funny, too.

Mrs Clarke always called her pupils

by their proper names. She didn't even shorten them. If your name was Samantha, that's what she'd call you, even if everyone else called you Ant.

But there was another reason I didn't want Mrs Clarke to be my teacher. It was because of something bad that happened last year.

I was playing rounders and I ran backwards to hit the ball. I didn't notice Mrs Clarke standing right behind me, and I knocked her over.

I mean, *completely* over.

I turned round and there she was, flat on her back, looking really surprised. I was worried she was hurt but she got up and brushed herself down.

'I'm sorry, Mrs Clarke,' I said nervously.

I thought she'd say something like, *That's OK, I know you didn't mean it*. That's what Mrs Khan would've said. But she didn't.

Instead she gave me a really mean look

and said, 'It's not a good idea to run back-wards.'

Then she walked off.

I knew then that Mrs Clarke didn't like me. It felt like there were two things that might happen this year – I might get Mr Stavros and have lots of fun or I might get Mrs Clarke and have no fun at all.

CHAPTER TWO

I woke up early the next morning – way before the alarm went off, and way before Ashley. I was excited.

Last year Dad used to drop me off at school but this year I was going to catch the bus with Dani. I didn't want to miss it, especially not on the first day. Ashley kept telling me the bus wasn't that great but I didn't care what she thought.

I was looking forward to it.

Ashley was waiting outside the shower when I got out.

'About time!' she said, which is funny, because she takes ten times longer than I do in the bathroom.

We used to be good friends but Ashley thinks she's too cool to hang out with me now she's at secondary school.

Back in my room, I got my school uniform out of the wardrobe. It was hanging next to my favourite skirt, the one with the glittery flowers. I wore my skirt all the time during the holidays. But today I was actually excited about putting on my uniform again, even though it doesn't glitter. I look much older in it.

Then I did my hair. I always do my own hair and I like making up new hairstyles. The one I thought of that day was pretty tricky and used lots of pins. I spent so long on it that I started to run out of time.

When I looked at the clock I got a fright. If I didn't hurry I was going to miss the bus. I rushed to the kitchen and ate my cereal really quickly. I knew Dani would be waiting for me at the bus stop.

'Slow down!' said Mum, smiling. 'You'll be sick.'

I slowed down a bit, but not much.

'I really don't want to miss the bus,' I explained.

Dad shook his head. 'Anyone would think you'd rather catch the bus to school than get a lift with me!' he said.

I gave him a hug. 'It was fun driving with you when I was little,' I said, because I didn't want him to feel bad.

Then I really had to go.

'See ya!' I called, running out of the door. But I had to come back in straight away – I'd forgotten my school bag.

Ashley rolled her eyes. You would think she never made mistakes!

Dani was already at the bus stop when I arrived. She looked excited.

'I think it's coming,' she said.

Sure enough, the school bus appeared around the corner and slowed to a stop. But the moment I got on, I wasn't sure I wanted to be there any more.

It was really crowded, and the other

kids all looked much older than us. It was really noisy too. Everyone was talking over the top of each other.

'There aren't any seats left,' I whispered to Dani, as we squeezed down the aisle. I wondered if it was too late to get a lift with Dad after all. But then Dani pointed.

'Look! There are two places,' she said, and dragged me to some spare seats right at the back of the bus.

We'd only been sitting down for a minute when the boy in front of us turned round. He stared at us like we were from another planet. Sometimes the older kids think they can boss everyone else around. They act like they're almost teachers.

Callum is like that.

'Don't you know the rules?' he said, giving us a really nasty look. 'No little kids at the back of the bus.'

Oh ... I don't think I like the bus!

I was ready to move straight away, but Dani wasn't. She didn't give up easily. She wasn't scared of anything, either. Big dogs, big kids, big storms. Nothing.

'We're not little kids,' she said. 'Little

kids aren't even allowed to catch the bus.'

Callum looked annoyed.

'If *I* say you're a little kid, then you *are* one,' he growled.

Everyone around us went quiet. They were waiting to see what would happen.

'Come on, Dani,' I muttered. 'There are some seats at the front.'

'Your friend's right,' Callum said to Dani. 'That's where the shrimps belong.'

'Well, then *you* should go up there,' replied Dani. 'I'm much taller than you!'

Everyone laughed then because it was true. Even though she was much younger than Callum, Dani was taller.

'Yeah, Callum,' one of his friends said.

'You should sit with all the little kids.'

Callum looked like he was worried someone really would make him move. 'No,' he said, crossing his arms. 'I'm not going anywhere.'

Everyone turned round and started talking again. It looked like we could stay!

I squeezed Dani's hand and thought for about the hundredth time how lucky I was to have her as my best friend.

CHAPTER THREE

It was weird when we arrived at school. Instead of going to our old building we walked right past it to our new area, called the Multi-Purpose Area.

There were already loads of kids waiting there. Dani and I soon spotted our gang – Nicole, Sarah and Annabelle.

It was excellent to see them again. We've been friends since the first day of school. People often ask if we are all sisters. This is pretty funny because we look totally different.

For example, Dani is tall with lots of freckles while Annabelle is short and has olive skin. But we think the same. One day we all turned up at school with our hair done in the same style! It was like we belonged to a secret hairstyle club. No one believed it was an accident.

We didn't have long to chat. The bell rang and our new teachers came in. Everyone went quiet.

Mr Stavros winked at us but Mrs Clarke didn't even smile. My friends and I all looked at each other. I knew we were all thinking the same thing — *I hope we're in Mr Stavros's class.*

Mr Stavros read out his class list.

Nicole's name got called.

Then Sarah's.

Then Annabelle's.

They went over to the left of the room looking happy. Dani and I were left on the right.

We were in Mrs Clarke's class, and our gang had been split up for the first time ever. I was glad that at least Dani and I were together.

The two classes left the area behind their new teachers. Already Mr Stavros's class was laughing at some joke he'd made. But our class was completely quiet.

Our classroom looked much bigger than Mrs Khan's did last year, and the walls were really bare. The first thing we had to do was choose a seat. Naturally, Dani and I sat together. Then Mrs Clarke started talking.

'You're not babies any more,' she said, 'so I don't want to see any baby behaviour.'

She told us the classroom rules.

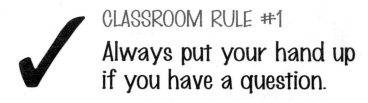

CLASSROOM RULE #1
Always put your hand up if you have a question.

CLASSROOM RULE #2
Don't leave your seat
without permission.

CLASSROOM RULE #3
Don't talk while the
teacher is talking.

Dani looked at me and pulled a face and I pulled one back. But we made sure Mrs Clarke didn't see. There was probably a rule about that too.

NEW CLASSROOM RULE
No pulling faces.

Next, Mrs Clarke had a surprise for us. But it wasn't a good one.

'We are going to have a maths test,' she said. 'I'll call out the sums. Write the answers down as quickly as you can.'

I couldn't believe it. We'd only been back at school for an hour and already we were having a maths test!

Through the wall I could hear Mr Stavros's class. He was playing his guitar and they were singing along. I could tell *they* weren't doing a test.

Mrs Clarke started calling out the questions. I knew the answer to the first one, but then they got harder and I started having trouble.

I looked around. Everyone else was scribbling down the answers.

As the test went on I started feeling sick. There were some questions that I thought I understood, but Mrs Clarke was going so fast I didn't have time to think.

It was terrible!

It looked like I was going to be handing in a piece of paper with hardly anything on it.

I looked at Dani. She was writing down the answers as quickly as Mrs Clarke called out the questions. Did I mention that, as well as being brave and funny, Dani was also really brainy?

I didn't want her to know I was having trouble with the test, so I started guessing. I just wrote down anything that came into my head and hoped that some of my answers would be right.

At the end Mrs Clarke collected our papers. Then she gave out some more sums to do for homework.

'That was easy!' said Dani, looking relieved. 'I thought maths was going to be hard this year.'

My stomach felt really weird – like I'd eaten a hot fudge sundae and done twenty spins in a row.

Dani knew something was wrong.

'Are you OK?' she asked. 'You look strange.'

I almost told her that I had found the maths test hard. But I didn't. Because if

I told her then she would know my terrible secret — I wasn't clever enough to be in this year.

CHAPTER FOUR

When the break-time bell finally rang, Dani and I went to meet the others in our new play area. Annabelle was at a music lesson, but Nicole and Sarah were talking about what a great morning they'd had. Even Mr Stavros's rules sounded good.

'If you do something wrong you have to do a *dead ant*,' said Nicole.

'What's that?' I asked.

'You lie on your back in front of everyone and wave your arms and legs in the air,' explained Nicole.

Dani and I laughed. That sounded funny. And really embarrassing.

Mrs Clarke would NEVER do that!

Mr Stavros had started teaching them all a song to perform at the first assembly of the year.

'And he said that we three could work

out a dance to do at the same time,' said Sarah, looking excited.

I couldn't help feeling a bit jealous. I wondered if Dani felt the same.

Last year our group used to make up dances every lunchtime and pretend we were on TV. We kept talking about how one day we would put on a concert. Now it looked like the others were going to do one without us.

It was worse for Dani – she was the best dancer out of all of us. If anyone should be doing a show, it was her. But she didn't look as though she minded.

The others couldn't believe it when we told them we'd already done a maths test.

'Mrs Clarke is really strict,' said Dani. 'But the work isn't all that hard.' Then she looked at me. 'The test was easy, wasn't it, Chloe?'

'It wasn't too bad,' I said, but I couldn't look at my friends as I said it.

What would they think if they knew the truth? They might not want me hanging around with them any more.

Dani started doing some dance steps. They were part of the routine we'd been working on together over the summer.

'That's so cool,' said Nicole, watching her. 'You're such a good dancer.'

It was true. Dani made dancing look easy. Her arms and legs always did exactly what her mind was thinking. My mind often had good ideas but the rest of me just couldn't keep up.

'Hey,' said Sarah, grabbing Nicole's arm. 'Maybe Dani could help us work out our dance for school assembly!'

'That's a great idea!' said Nicole. She looked at Dani. 'Would you do that?'

Dani shrugged. 'Yes. Why not?' she said.

And then it was like they completely forgot about me. Dani started showing Nicole and Sarah different steps while I just sat on the grass and watched.

I couldn't help feeling a bit cross. And the more I watched, the more cross I felt. Many of the steps that Dani taught them were from our own dance. Some of them were even ones I'd made up!

I couldn't understand why Dani wanted to help them so much when we weren't even going to be in the show.

I was getting really bored when Annabelle arrived from her music lesson. She had news.

'I just heard Mr Stavros talking to Mrs Clarke in the corridor,' she said. 'Mrs Clarke said, "If she doesn't settle in soon she'll have to be moved".'

'Who was she talking about?' asked Dani.

Annabelle shrugged. 'I didn't hear that bit, but it sounds like they're planning to get rid of someone,' she said.

'Or maybe move them down a class,' suggested Sarah. 'They do that sometimes when a kid has trouble keeping up.'

The others started guessing who the

teachers might've meant. Maybe it was Dale, who was the youngest in the class. Or maybe it was the new girl, Stephanie.

I kept quiet because I already knew who it was.

Me.

Mrs Clarke must have seen my test already. She must have realised that I wasn't clever enough to keep up with the others. I knew that it wouldn't be long before I was put back into my old class.

CHAPTER FIVE

After break Mrs Clarke got us to write a story about our holidays. Lots of kids groaned but I was happy. I like writing stories, even if teachers keep asking us to write about the same things. I think I've written a story about my holidays every year since I started school!

When we finished, Mrs Clarke clapped her hands.

'Now we are going to choose this week's monitors,' she said.

Dani was chosen as lunch monitor and I was made pet monitor.

Pet monitor sounded like a good job. And it would've been OK if I was in Mr Stavros's class – their class pet is a terrapin called Boris. Terrapins are cute. But our class pets are two hermit crabs called Snippy and Snappy. They remind me of spiders, but they are worse than spiders because they have claws.

Mrs Clarke got us to sit on the mat in a circle.

'Chloe,' said Mrs Clarke, 'please bring Snippy and Snappy over here.'

I felt like saying, *Do I have to?* but I didn't think Mrs Clarke would like that very much. So I went over and took the lid off the crabs' tank. They were crawling around on the rocks. I wished I had a pair of gloves.

I reached in and picked up Snippy, who went into his shell. At first Snappy did the same thing when I picked her up.

It wasn't so bad carrying them like that but I still walked as quickly as I could.

Just as I was about to put them down Snappy darted a claw out and nipped my finger.

'Ow!' I yelled, and dropped her on the ground. She rolled around for a moment

and then started running across the carpet,
right towards me!

Maybe it wasn't the best thing to do,
but I screamed and jumped up on a chair.

I know hermit crabs aren't dangerous but I still didn't like being chased by one.

'Chloe is scared of a tiny little crab!' said Matt, and the whole class laughed at me. Mrs Clarke picked up Snappy.

'Can I hold her, Mrs Clarke?' asked Dani.

Mrs Clarke put Snappy into Dani's hand. I waited for Snappy to nip her, but she didn't. She just sat there quietly and didn't even try to run away.

'She's so sweet!' said Dani, stroking Snappy's shell with one finger. I felt a bit cross when Dani did that. It made me look like a chicken.

'Snappy's frightened,' said Mrs Clarke. 'Think what it's like for her – a tiny little crab surrounded by all these giants.'

I felt a bit sorry for Snappy then, but I still didn't want to go near her again.

'Maybe Dani and I could swap monitor jobs?' I suggested, hopefully.

But Mrs Clarke shook her head.

'No,' she said, putting Snappy back in my hand. 'You're pet monitor for the week, Chloe. No swapping.'

I sighed, but there was no point arguing with someone like Mrs Clarke. You'd have more luck arguing with Snappy.

CHAPTER SIX

By the end of the lesson I needed to go to the toilet. I mean, I was really bursting! But I didn't want to ask Mrs Clarke if I could go. Every time I spoke I seemed to do something wrong.

I knew it would be lunchtime soon, so I just held on. But when you need to go to the toilet time passes very slowly. It felt like hours before we finally heard the bell ring.

'I'll meet you later,' I said to Dani, and rushed off to the loo.

In our building last year the girls' toilets were on the left and the boys' were on the right. So I rushed into the toilets on the left without even looking at the sign on the door.

That was a big mistake.

At first I couldn't work out what was going on. There was a boy standing at the basin. We stared at each other. He looked as shocked to see me as I was to see him.

'What are you doing in the girls' toilets?' I asked.

'No,' he said, 'what are *you* doing in the *boys'* toilets?'

Then another boy walked in and I realised it *was* me who had made the mistake.

I ran out of there as fast as I could,
hoping no one else would see me. But
unfortunately on the way out I ran into
Matt. He was very surprised to see me.

Then he guessed what I'd done.

'I can't wait to tell everyone about this!' he said, grinning.

I tried to think what Dani would do.

'You'd better not tell anyone,' I said, putting on a really mean face. 'Or else!' But I could tell Matt wasn't scared of me.

I was right. By the time I found my friends everyone knew what had happened. News like that spreads pretty quickly around our playground.

'That must have been *so* awful,' said Sarah. 'I would've died!'

'It's not that bad,' said Dani. 'I bet it happens all the time.'

Dani always made me feel better. But I couldn't help feeling that the rest of my friends were starting to look at me strangely. Like I was a bit embarrassing to be around.

So I made a vow.

No more messing up, I told myself.

It seemed to work, because I managed to get through the rest of the day without making any more mistakes.

Dani and I caught the bus home toge-ther and got the same seats we'd had in the morning. No one said anything about it this time, either.

'Do you want to come over for a swim?' I asked as we got off the bus.

Dani shook her head. 'I'd better not,' she said. 'We've got that maths homework to do.'

I'd forgotten about that.

'We could go for a swim first,' I said, 'and then do the homework together. It wouldn't take long.'

But Dani had made up her mind.

'See you tomorrow!' she said, opening her front gate.

I went straight to my room and put my swimming costume on. I couldn't wait to dive into the pool. Diving always makes me feel better. Mum was in the sitting room.

'No homework?' she asked as I headed outside.

'I'll do it later,' I said. I decided I would just do a few dives and then I would do my homework.

But once I started diving I forgot all about my maths homework. I did a normal dive and then a couple of backwards ones. Then I did some somersaults.

It felt good plunging into the cool water over and over again. I stopped thinking about Mrs Clarke and about walking into the wrong toilets.

I stopped worrying about being pet monitor. I even stopped caring about being moved down a grade. I just thought about keeping my toes pointed and my chin tucked in.

CHAPTER
SEVEN

When I woke up the next morning I felt sick. Not properly sick though, just *worried* sick. It was because of the maths homework.

Last night it'd seemed like a good idea not to do it. Now I wasn't so sure. I got up and found the questions in my bag. Maybe they would be easy, and I could get them done before school.

I tried. I tried really, really hard. But I just couldn't work out the sums.

None of my answers looked right and every time I tried again I got a different answer. It was hopeless. I would never be able to work them out, even if I kept trying for a hundred years.

Dani knew me pretty well. When we got on the bus together she could tell that something was wrong.

'Did you do your maths homework?' she asked.

'No,' I said, pretending I didn't care.

'I didn't feel like it.'

Dani stared at me. 'You'll get in to trouble when Mrs Clarke finds out,' she said.

That made me cross. She was right but I didn't want to think about it. When I get cross I sometimes say nasty things. I don't mean to – they just pop out.

'So what?' I said, shrugging my shoulders. 'Only goody-goodies do homework.'

'I did *my* homework,' Dani said.

'Well, then, you're a goody-goody,' I replied.

'No, I'm not,' she said.

'Yes, you are,' I said. 'You're the favourite. You're the teacher's pet.'

Dani went red.

'I am *not*!' she said. She was almost yelling.

'Teacher's pet. Teacher's pet,' I chanted.

I knew I was being mean, but I didn't care.

Callum turned around. He'd heard

what I was chanting, and even though he didn't know why I was saying it, he started saying it too.

'Teacher's pet. Teacher's pet.'

Before long it seemed like everyone on the bus was chanting. Dani put her hands over her ears and screwed up her eyes. It got so loud that finally the bus driver yelled at everyone to be quiet.

Dani took her hands from her ears but wouldn't look at me.

I started to feel terrible.

I knew I'd really hurt her feelings.

We went the rest of the way without speaking. I sat there trying to think of what I could say to make it up to Dani. But everything I thought of sounded stupid.

I thought about pretending it had all been a joke. That wouldn't work though – you don't play mean jokes on your friends.

I knew that I should tell her how sorry I was and hope she'd forgive me.

I decided I would apologise to her as soon as we got off the bus. But I didn't get a chance. The moment the bus doors opened, Dani jumped up and ran off.

'Dani! Wait!' I called.

But she didn't hear me. Or maybe she just didn't want to hear me.

I knew what Dani would do. She'd go and find the others and tell them what I had done. Then they would all be mad at me. I knew I should find her as soon as possible to try and make things right, but I was supposed to go and look after the hermit crabs before class.

Great! Things were just getting better and better. I couldn't believe that I had actually been looking forward to going back to school.

CHAPTER EIGHT

I knocked on the classroom door. Mrs Clarke was sitting at her desk.

'Excuse me, Mrs Clarke,' I said. 'I have to look after the crabs.'

'Go ahead,' she said, without looking up.

She sounded grumpy, as usual.

I tried to imagine Mrs Clarke laughing. Or even smiling!

There was an ice-cream container next

to the tank to put the crabs in while their water was changed. I decided to pick up Snippy first. He disappeared into his shell straight away. Then it was Snappy's turn. As my hand came closer she started waving her claws around like she couldn't wait to nip me again.

'She's only doing that because she's scared of you,' said Mrs Clarke. She was watching me from her desk.

Well, I thought, *I'm scared of her, too. And I don't have great big claws.*

Mrs Clarke came over and picked Snappy up.

'Look at her shell,' she said.

I looked closely at Snappy for the first time. Her shell was really beautiful – smooth and white and curled up like a spiral. I hadn't noticed it before.

'Hermit crabs don't have shells of their own,' explained Mrs Clarke. 'They just walk around until they find one that they like the look of.'

'Like going shopping!' I said.

It was funny to think of crabs shopping. It made them seem like people.

Mrs Clarke nodded.

'Exactly,' she said. 'When she's too big for this shell we'll put some new ones in her tank and see which one she chooses.'

I started thinking about the shell I'd choose if I were a crab. Something really pointy, with yellow stripes, maybe.

Mrs Clarke put Snappy back in the ice-cream container.

'If I were a hermit crab,' she said, 'I'd choose a pointy shell with yellow stripes.'

I stared at her in surprise. 'Me, too!' I said.

'We must have the same taste in shells,' said Mrs Clarke.

And then something really weird happened. Mrs Clarke actually smiled at me.

The bell rang. I finished cleaning the tank as quickly as I could.

Dani arrived and sat down without looking at me. I had forgotten about our fight. Now I felt awful all over again.

The first class was maths and Mrs Clarke wrote some sums on the board. They were the same sort as the ones she'd given us for homework, but even harder.

Mrs Clarke showed us how to do the first one and I listened carefully. I thought that maybe this time I understood.

'Work through the rest of these,' said Mrs Clarke, 'and put up your hand if you have trouble.'

Everyone started working quietly.

I looked at the first question. But even though I had listened carefully, I couldn't do it. I looked around the room to see if anyone else was asking for help. No one was so I didn't want to put my hand up either.

I started feeling really worried. So I did the same thing I'd done the day before – I just wrote down any old numbers.

All that was bad enough, but things got worse. At the end of the lesson Mrs Clarke came around and collected our homework. When she got to me she stopped.

'Where's yours, Chloe?' she asked.

'I didn't do it,' I said.

Mrs Clarke raised an eyebrow. 'Why not?' she asked.

I thought about saying, *I didn't feel like it*, like I'd said to Dani. But I knew that wouldn't be such a good idea.

'I don't know,' I mumbled, staring at my desk. Everyone was staring at me. 'I just didn't.'

'Please stay behind at lunchtime, Chloe,' said Mrs Clarke, quietly.

And then she walked away.

CHAPTER nine

The next class went really slowly. All I could think about was what Mrs Clarke was going to say to me at lunchtime.

Everyone left when the lunch bell rang. Everyone except me. I stayed in my seat. Dani left without looking at me.

Suddenly the room was very quiet.

It was so quiet that I could even hear the sound of Mrs Clarke's pen scratching on her page as she worked at her desk.

My stomach felt strange again, like I had the whole ocean swirling around inside me. There were little fish darting around in there, and a shark that kept bumping into my chest.

Outside the window I could see my friends practising their dance routine. They were getting pretty good at it.

I wished I was out there with them. In fact, I wished this whole morning had never happened.

Finally, Mrs Clarke came over and sat down beside me. I was pretty sure I knew what she was going to say. She would say that I couldn't stay in her class any more.

She might even send me to the head-mistress because I hadn't done my homework. But the weird thing was, I didn't really mind.

I didn't even care about being moved down a grade. Last year I really liked school. The work was easy and I felt clever.

I don't care if I get moved down a grade!

This year all that had changed. And my friends would hate me once they found out what I'd said to Dani. If I got moved down a grade, I might be able to start all over again.

So when Mrs Clarke asked me why I didn't do my homework, I decided to tell her the truth.

'Because I didn't know how to,' I said.

I showed her the page I had worked on that morning before school. It was a mess of numbers and crossed-out lines.

I waited for Mrs Clarke to get cross. I thought she might tell me it wasn't hard, and that all the other kids could do it. But she didn't say that at all.

Instead she nodded.

'This type of maths can be hard to

understand,' she said. 'Not everyone can do it straight away. Let's go through it together.'

Then she started explaining it again. But although I really wanted to understand, I just didn't. Mrs Clarke was wasting her time.

'Does this make sense?' she said, after a while. I shook my head.

'No,' I said. 'I still don't get it.'

'Which bits don't you understand?' asked Mrs Clarke. She didn't say it in an angry way, though. She said it in a kind way.

I think it was because she was being nice that I started to cry. Yes, I burst into tears right there, in front of Mrs Clarke.

I couldn't help myself.

'I don't understand *any* of it!' I said. 'I'm not smart enough. I want to go back to my old class.'

It was a big relief just to say it out loud.

Mrs Clarke gave me some tissues.

'Everyone finds some things hard,

Chloe,' she said. 'You find maths hard, but you find other things easy.'

I shook my head.

'I don't find *anything* easy,' I said.

Mrs Clarke put a piece of paper in front of me. It was my story from yesterday. There were two big ticks at the top!

'This is a really good story, Chloe,' said Mrs Clarke. 'In fact, I want you to read it out in assembly next week.'

I kept staring at the two ticks. Ashley had told me that Mrs Clarke never gave anyone more than one tick.

But writing wasn't like maths.

'Anyone can write a story,' I said.

Mrs Clarke shook her head.

'No, lots of people find it really difficult. Just as difficult as you are finding this new maths.'

I'd never thought that I might be good at writing. It made me feel a bit better. But I still felt mostly bad.

'I don't think I'll ever understand this maths,' I said.

Mrs Clarke pointed to a sentence in my story.

'You wrote here that you like diving,' she said. 'I bet you found that hard when you first started.'

I was going to tell Mrs Clarke that was not true at all. It felt like I'd always found diving easy. But then I remembered what it was like in the beginning. I did lots of belly-flops that really hurt.

Once I slipped on the edge of the pool and got a bloody nose.

And then I remembered what it was like when I did my first proper dive. I knew even before I jumped that this time it wouldn't be a belly-flop.

It had felt great!

Was it possible that the same thing could happen with maths? I didn't really think it could, but perhaps it was worth trying.

'Can you show me again, Mrs Clarke?'
I said.

She nodded. 'Of course,' she said.

So Mrs Clarke explained the maths again, right from the beginning. And this time, finally, I understood! The moment I got it, the ocean inside my stomach disappeared, like someone had pulled out a plug and the water had all drained away.

But there was still something I wanted to know.

'Mrs Clarke, were you going to put me into another grade if I didn't work this stuff out?'

Mrs Clarke was surprised.

'No! I hadn't thought about doing that at all,' she said. 'I knew you would understand it in the end.'

'But Annabelle heard you say that someone would be moved if they didn't settle in soon,' I said.

Mrs Clarke looked puzzled for a moment. And then she laughed.

'I wasn't talking about *you*,' she said. 'I was talking about Snappy! We got her a new tank and she doesn't seem to like it. We might have to get her a different one.'

I must admit I felt pretty silly.

But I didn't mind, not one little bit. For once I was actually glad I had made a mistake!

CHAPTER TEN

There wasn't much of lunchtime left by the time I'd finished talking to Mrs Clarke. I had to hurry. There was something else I needed to do before the bell rang.

I ran as fast as I could to where my friends were practising. They stopped when they saw me coming and looked at me without smiling – like they weren't even my friends any more.

Dani started to walk away when she saw me, but I grabbed her arm. I had to say this right now.

'Dani, I'm really sorry about what happened this morning,' I said.

I said it loudly so the others could hear me too. 'It was the stupidest thing I've ever done. Ever. And I know you might never forgive me. But I promise never to do anything like that again and I really hope we can be friends again.'

Annabelle had her arms crossed. 'What you said to Dani was really mean,' she said.

'And it wasn't even true,' added Nicole. 'She's not the teacher's pet.'

'I know she's not,' I said. 'I don't know why I said it.'

'You should do something to show how sorry you are,' said Sarah.

She was right. I wanted to show Dani that I knew what an idiot I'd been. But what could I do to show her?

And then I had an idea.

Not the greatest idea, but an idea all the same. I lay on the ground and waggled my arms and legs in the air. My friends stared at me, wondering what I was doing. Then Nicole started laughing.

'She's doing a dead ant!' she said.

'You're getting grass and stuff in your hair,' said Annabelle, giggling.

But I didn't care.

I kept on doing the dead ant.

At first Dani wouldn't even look at me.

She pretended there was something really

interesting happening on the sports field.

But after a while she couldn't help

sneaking a look. And I saw her start to smile, even though she tried to hide it.

'You don't look anything like a dead ant,' she said. 'You look more like a puppy that wants its tummy scratched.'

I knew then that Dani had started to forgive me. I was so glad! It was horrible to think that I'd almost lost my best friend.

I decided there and then that I would never let anything like that happen again.

CHAPTER ELEVEN

On the day of the school assembly Dani and I made sure we had a seat in the front row. After all the announcements were over, Mr Stavros got up on stage with his guitar and his class stood behind him. At the front of the class were our friends!

When the music started, they all started to sing. Annabelle, Sarah and Nicole began to dance.

It was strange to see them dancing some of the steps I had made up. I thought I'd feel jealous that it wasn't me up there, but I didn't feel jealous at all. Instead, I was proud. They weren't bad steps!

'They're such good dancers,' I whispered to Dani.

My friends are fantastic!

She nodded. 'They are good, but we're good, too. Maybe Mrs Clarke will let us do our own dance in assembly one week,' she said.

Once I would've thought that there was no way Mrs Clarke would let us do that. But I knew her better now.

I nodded. 'Let's ask her,' I said.

Our friends only made a couple of small mistakes. Annabelle nearly tripped over at the start and Sarah spun to the left instead of to the right. But she did a good job of covering it up and I think only we noticed.

When they finished, everyone in the audience went crazy! Kids were jumping around and cheering. I even saw some of them trying to copy the moves themselves.

It was really funny.

Then it was my turn to read out my story. Watching the dance, I had forgotten all about it and had stopped feeling nervous. But once I stood up on stage, in front of all those faces, I started to feel nervous again. Then I told myself it was just like diving.

I looked at the page and imagined I was standing on the edge of a pool, getting ready to plunge into the water. And when I started reading, my voice didn't wobble at all.

Everyone was very quiet while I read my story. I couldn't tell if they liked it or not until I finished and everyone clapped.

They clapped a lot, especially Mrs Clarke! Someone in the front row was cheering and whistling really loudly.

It was Dani.

And sitting beside her were Annabelle, Nicole and Sarah, cheering just as loudly.

It had been a bit of a rough start, but now I knew it was going to be a good year.

If you loved this GO GIRL!
story, why not look for the
others in the series, available
in all good bookshops.

For more information,
go to our website at
www.egmont.co.uk